Ian Brady

The Mo

What you are about to read are ๛om real life events. Nothing contained in this short story is fiction.

Everything you will read are are based on facts. Please have caution when reading through this story as some of the content will be disturbing. If you are easily offended, then please do not read the contents of this story.

If you find the following content worthy of a review, not only would I be very grateful but it will help me in my writing journey for the future.

Thank You

Contents:

- <u>Public hatred</u>

- <u>Return to the Moors</u>

The Moors Murderers

Some crimes are so terrible that they become national nightmares, and the Moors Murderers have remained in the headlines for longer than most.

Ian Brady and Myra Hindley killed for kicks. The couple met in 1961 while working for a Manchester chemical firm. She was a 19-year old typist; he was a 23-year old stock clerk. The pair became lovers and developed a sick mutual thrill from killing innocent youngsters virtually without motive.

Brady was born in Glasgow, the illegitimate son of a waitress. He never knew his father and was brought up by foster parents in the tough poverty-ridden tenements of the Gorbals.

Hindley was a local girl, born and brought up in the industrial suburb of Gorton. She was average in every way and failed to do well at school. In her early teens she tool to the Catholic faith, regularly attending Mass.

When they met, Brady was well on the way to being a full-blown psychopath. He had a private library of books about torture and ritual killing, his favourite being the works of the Maquis de Sade.

Hindley was quickly influenced and dominated by her older boyfriend, whom she regarded as an intellectual genius. She soon took an avid interest in his books on leather fetishism, sexual sadism and bondage, at a time when pornography was generally hard to obtain.

Brady decided he would become a bank robber. Unable to get a gun licence because he had a criminal record, he persuaded his lover to join a shooting club at Cheadle in Cheshire. From her contacts there she was able to buy two unlicensed pistols, a Webley .45 and a Smith & Wesson .38.

Brady would take them to the moors above Manchester for target practice with Hindley's teenage brother-in-law David Smith, whom he hoped to corrupt and make his partner in robbery.

By 1963 Brady was talking openly about his fascination with committing the perfect murder. On 12 July he told Hindley, now totally obedient to him, that the time had come.

They made plans to tour the side-streets of the Manchester suburbs to find someone to kill. It didn't matter if it was male or female. As long as the victim was young, Brady would be happy.

Searching for victims

Hindley was to cruise the residential roads in a borrowed van while Brady followed on his motorbike. When he spotted a likely victim he would flash his lights as a signal. Hindley was to stop and lure the victim into the van on the promise of a reward for helping her find an expensive glove lost at a picnic on the moors a few days before.

Brady flashed his lights as they passed 16-year old Pauline Reade, whom Hindley knew was a local girl. But despite the fact that Hindley was on speaking terms with the doomed girl's mother, she lured her into the van. After driving a short distance, she offered to give her some pop records as payment if she would come and help her look for the lost glove. Pauline was on her way to a Saturday night dance but, being good natured and friendly, she agreed to help.

Trip to the moors

They drove to the moors and pulled into a lay-by at Hollin Brow Knoll, a beauty spot popular with courting couples and picnickers. There Hindley introduced Pauline to Brady as her boyfriend. Brady told Hindley to drive the van further on to a better parking place while he and Pauline walked on to the moor away from the road to start the search. There Brady suddenly sexually assaulted the off-guard teenager, then slashed her throat with a knife.

In her confession 24 years later Myra Hindley told police that Brady had returned to the van and asked her to follow him back on to the moor. There she saw Pauline, her skirt pulled up and underwear undone, bleeding to death.

She said: "I could see lots of blood and Pauline was making a strange gurgling noise. I felt sick, I wanted to go away."

Brady told Hindley to wait with the stricken girl and walked away. He returned a few minutes later with a spade he had hidden in a drainage ditch several days before.

By then Pauline was dead. Ordering Hindley back to the van, Brady set about burying the still-clothed body of Pauline Reade in a makeshift grave. Brady later returned to the van with the spade and the knife. He loaded his motorcycle into the back of the van and the couple drove away from the scene of their first dreadful deed.

Ian Brady: The making of a sadist

Ian Brady lived with foster parents in the tough tenements of Glasgow. By the age of 16 he was a chain-smoker and heavy drinker, and was well on his way to a life of crime. He had been arrested several times for theft and assault, and had a disturbing reputation for bullying younger children.

He moved to Manchester, but his new environment produced no change in Brady. When he was 18, Brady was placed in a special Borstal unit for offenders of above-average intelligence, but when he was caught making alcohol in a home-made still he was transferred to a much tougher Borstal in Hull, from where he emerged a totally warped character.

By the time he met Hindley, he was a 23-year old clerk. A self-avowed Nazi, he could quote long passages from *Mein Kampf*. He was also fascinated by sadism. One of his favourite books was Compulsion, about the kidnap and murder of a 12-year old by the wealthy young Americans Leopold and Loeb.

What made Myra a monster?

Myra Hindley came from Gorton, an industrial suburb of Manchester. She was attracted to religion, and became a regular churchgoer at her local Roman Catholic church. However, all that changed when Myra met Ian Brady.

Brady completed dominated the impressionable 19-year old. Myra thought that Brady was a genius, and she needed no prompting to embrace her lover's sick appetites, rejecting her Catholicism and the conventions of family and marriage.

Myra bleached her hair blonde and posed in jackboots as Nazi prison-camp guard Irma Grese, the 'Beast of Belsen'. She also posed for crude pornographic pictures. By the time her twisted lover began to act out his murderous fantasies, Myra was his willing accomplice.

Destroying the evidence

Back at the house they shared in the slum area of Gorton, Brady burned the clothes he had been wearing on the fire grate, cleaned the spade and tried to destroy the kitchen knife he had used to kill Pauline. When it wouldn't break he took it out and threw it off a bridge into a brook near Macclesfield.

During the clean-up operation Brady told his lover that he had found four half crowns in Pauline's coat pocket and had taken them and spent them on cigarettes and sweets. At this time the death penalty was still in force for murder committed during robbery. Hindley, terrified she might hang if they were ever found out, insisted they return to the murder scene the next day. In a bizarre act they scattered four half crowns of their own in the long grass alongside where Pauline lay cold in the wet ground.

Another murder

By November Brady was tingling with the urge to kill again. He told Hindley: "It is time to do another."

They hired a white Ford Anglia on Saturday 23 November and set off to look for another victim to slaughter. After driving around for several hours they returned home and Brady loaded a spade and an unlicensed .22 rifle into the boot of the car.

Hindley put on a black wig and a head scarf, fearing that her bleached blonde hair might later identify her if they were spotted abducting a youngster from the street.

They drive to a market place in Ashton-under-Lyne. There they spotted 12-year old John Kilbride who was buying six pennyworth of broken biscuits from a stall.

Brady approached the boy and asked him if he would like to have some sherry. The boy happily clambered into the front passenger seat next to Hindley while Brady got into the back. They drove towards the moors.

Using the old ruse of a lost glove, Brady asked the wide-eyed 12-year old to help with the search.

Lured out of sight

Fetching a torch and the spade from the boot Brady told his lover to drive away, park in the nearby village of Greenfield, and return for them in half an hour. Then, ushering little John to the side of the road they set off across the rough ground and out of sight down a slope.

There Brady had suddenly attacked the boy. He later told Hindley that he had intended to stab the boy using a knife with a six-inch blade, but when he had come to use it found it was too blunt for the job. Instead he pulled a length of string from his pocket and strangled the crying child.

After sexually assaulting the boy Brady set to work digging another grave in the boggy soil.

After finishing his ghoulish work, Brady found he had forgotten to put in one of his victim's shoes, lost in his desperate struggle for life, and took it back to the car with him.

The missing shoe

Two years later when John Kilbride's remains were found, detectives were baffled as to why he was only wearing one shoe.

Back at home that night the boy's shoe was burned along with the clothes Brady had worn that day. The knife and string were destroyed and the spade cleaned. A major police investigation followed the disappearance of John Kilbride. There were newspaper and television appeals. Experienced detectives were sure he had been abducted and murdered.

A huge operation to question thousands of shoppers from the market where he was last seen was mounted, but no clues to his disappearance were found. For several days the murderous couple were anxious when police organised a huge search of moorland near Greenfield where Hindley had parked on the fatal evening, but the hunt was called off a mile short of where John's body lay in a shallow grave.

In early 1964 Brady and Hindley brought an Austin A40 and later part-exchanged it for a Mini pick-up. By June Brady said he wanted to kill yet again. The twisted couple set off looking for a new target.

On 16 June they found what they were looking for, another schoolboy. They were driving along a turning off Stockport Road when they spotted Keith Bennett. Brady, in the back of the pick-up, tapped on the rear glass, the signal for Hindley to stop.

The story they had rehearsed this time was that they wanted some help to move heavy boxes from a shop. Keith Bennett, a good natured boy of 12 with a Beatle hair cut and thick glasses, happily jumped into the passenger seat alongside Hindley.

After a short distance Brady ordered his girlfriend to stop and asked the lad to get into the back of the pick-up with him. Keith happily compiled.

The pick-up headed for Saddleworth Moor and stopped at a point known as How Grain. The glove ruse was used again to get Keith to make his final walk to death across the hammocks of heather and bracken on the deserted moor.

This time there was a variation in routine. Brady took his camera with him instead of driving away, Hindley locked the pick-up and followed a short distance behind carrying a pair of binoculars. They followed the course of a stream, known as Shiny Brook, until they were out of sight and earshot of the road. There Brady stopped and signalled to Hindley to use the binoculars to check for any possible witnesses.

When she gave the all-clear signal, Brady and the boy disappeared into a dip and Hindley sat down to wait. After about half an hour her man reappeared, alone. He was carrying a spade. He had hidden it on the moor days before as part of his preparation for the killing.

Strangled to death

Brady told her he had strangled Keith with a piece of string, then candidly told her he had sexually assaulted him. He had then dug a deep hole and buried him.

He had also taken sickening pictures of his young victim seconds after death. Brady developed the film at home and showed his lover the pictures. In her confession 23 years later Hindley told detectives: "the boy was lying on his back … there was blood on him so I wouldn't look closely. I couldn't say if he was alive or dead when the pictures were taken."

The next day the couple went to work as if nothing unusual had happened.

On Boxing Day 1964 wickedness had welled up once more in Brady and he told his lover they should find another victim. A fairground in the Miles Platting district of Manchester seemed to offer a good opportunity. It was there there, with Hindley once again wearing her ill-fitting dark-wig disguise, they they spotted 10-year old Lesley Ann watching the dodgem cars.

House of Horror

The Moors Murderers took their first victims out on to Saddleworth Moor to commit their crimes, the remote location making it very unlikely that anybody would catch them in the act. At the end of 1964, however, Brady and Hindley moved into a council house in Hattersley, Manchester, which has since been demolished. To all outward appearances it was a normal dwelling place, but with Brady and Hindley living there it became a house of horror.

Now they could murder in comfort, and as long as they gagged their victims the unsuspecting neighbours would never know what was happening on their very doorsteps. The moors were still close by for the disposal of the remains.

Little Lesley Ann was the fist person to be killed in the house, but it was the death of Edward Evans in the same place that was their downfall. His butchered body was still in the spare bedroom when investigators came to make their enquiries after David Smith's confession to the police.

Help with parcels

Brady and Hindley were carrying boxes to look as if they were holding Christmas gifts or shopping. Checking first to see if she was waiting for anyone to get off the rides, they made their approach. Lesley had in fact gone to the fair with her tow younger brothers. But they had got separated in the crowds. Now she was all alone.

As they walked close to her Hindley dropped her parcels on the floor and asked little Lesley to help her pick them up and carry them to their car. The child was happy to oblige. At the car they asked her if she would come home with them and help them unload. Again dark-haired Lesley, showing not the slightest suspicion of the strangers, agreed to help and got in the car.

What took place in the following hours represents some of the most diabolical acts In the annals of crime and detection. The couple had recently moved to a new house on a large council overspill estate in the Manchester suburb of Hattersley. In the bedroom Brady had already set up not only his camera and lighting equipment, but also a tape recorder. He wanted to record the sounds of a child's torture and death as well as the sights.

Hindley asked Lesley to carry the boxes upstairs to the room where Brady had already gone.

Begged for her life

Once there Brady pounced on the girl and tried to tear off her clothes. The tape recorder was running and the plaintive cries of Lesley asking him to stop, begging him not to hurt her, as he forced her to strip and to pose for pornographic pictures of the vilest nature, are burned into the memories of all who have heard them. Brady had forced a handkerchief into her mouth to muffle her cries.

Police were later to find a series of pictures of Lesley naked save for her shoes and socks and with a scarf wound round her face by Brady in a crude attempt to mask her identity. He had planned to peddle the pictures to child sex perverts.

At the end of the terrifying photo session Brady told Hindley to run a hot bath so they could "clean the girl up".

Hindley later told detectives that she waited in the bathroom for about 20 minutes and when Brady didn't bring the girl in she went back to the bedroom to be confronted by a horrific sight. Lesley Ann Downey was lying half on and half off the bed; Brady had raped and strangled her.

It was Boxing Day night. It was very quiet and bitterly cold. As they drove towards their burial ground on Saddleworth Moor the weather got worse. They ran into a blizzard and were forced to turn back when the road ahead was blocked by cars trapped in the drifting snow. They returned home and took the body of Lesley in again. Brady, blood still on his hands feverishly set about developing the pictures of the bestial session with the girl. The next day gritting lorries had been out. The Mini with its pathetic cargo was able to make it to Saddleworth Moor. There Brady lifted out the tiny corpse and sprinted into the darkness towards Hollin Brow Knoll, close to where Pauline Reade had been buried.

Describing the Lesley case years later, Hindley told police: "She went with us like a lamb to the slaughter. All the children did. When they saw a woman with Ian they lost all fear. They were sure nothing evil would happen to them if they were with a woman as well as a man."

It was the Moors Murderers fifth murder that was to bring them down. By October 1965 Brady was feeling the pangs of the killing urge once more. But this one as to be different. This was not to be about sexual gratification or the need to dominate anyone directly. This was to be more subtle.

A new accomplice

Once again the choice of victim was to be incidental. But the aim behind it was to be far more devious. This was to be an act of bonding between Brady and another young man he wanted to have complete power over, Hindley's 17-year old brother-in-law, David Smith.

Smith had married Myra's younger sister Maureen, who was 19, when she fell pregnant. The baby had died in infancy. Over the previous year the two couples had spent much time together.

Smith was another violent tearaway with several convictions for wounding, theft, and burglary already under his belt. This impressive young delinquent was in awe of Brady, whom he thought was smart, sophisticated, daring, an accomplished criminal who had guns and bragged about his plans for his spectacular robberies.

Brady was turned on my Smith's adulation. He took him to the moors to practice with revolvers and fantasise about the big stick-ups they planned to do. Brady boasted to him that he had already killed, telling him how easy it was. Now Brady decided to drag Smith into a plot that would give him power over him forever. He would implicate Smith in a murder.

On 6 October 1965 Brady decided to pick a young apprentice, Edward Evans, in a bar in central Manchester and bring him back to the house in Hattersley for the evening. The plot was to get Smith back to the house at the same time, murder the unfortunate Evans in front of him to implicate him, and make him subservient to Brady for ever.

Savage attack

Hindley lured Smith back to the house by saying Brady had laid in several bottles of wine for him. At the house he witnessed a scene of unmitigated savagery. As he waited in the kitchen he suddenly heard a terrible scream from the living room. Then he heard Myra shout: "Dave, help him." Thinking it as Brady who was under attack he rushed into the room to see Ian Brady raining blows upon a blood-soaked young stranger with a hand axe.

Smith was later to tell the police: "It was a horrible scene. The lad was screaming and trying to get away. Ian just kept hitting him with terrible blows to the head, neck and shoulders with the axe.

"I was frightened to death; my stomach was churning. There was blood everywhere, on the walls, the fireplace, all over."

Eventually Brady finished the job by strangling Evans with a length of electric flex. Then he turned to Hindley, who had witnessed the whole attack, and said: "Well, it's done. It's the messiest yet. Normally it only takes one blow."

Brady then told smith to help him clear up the mess. They carried Evans upstairs in a plastic sheet.

As they did so, Brady laughed and made jokes. He quipped: "Eddie's dead weight, isn't he?" Then, peering into the dreadful gashes in the man's skull, he joked: "He sure is brainy, isn't he?"

When they got the dead man into a spare room Brady again told Smith how he was surprised it had taken so long to despatch Evans.

"I mean, just feeling the weight of that," he said, handing Smith the axe. Smith was naïve, but not a complete fool. He realised he was the victim of a set-up. Brady was now trying to get Smith's fingerprints on the axe, too, to fully implicate him.

Brady said the body should be taken to Saddleworth Moor to be buried straight away. But in the ferocity of the attack, he had sprained his ankle and he told Smith to be back to help him with the job of disposal the next day.

Smith, now in sheer terror and convinced Brady might fly at him with the hatchet at any moment, decided on a desperate plan. He ran home and woke his wife, Myra's sister Maureen. At 6.10 the next morning police received a 999 call from a phone box on the council estate at Hattersley. Five minutes later a patrol car pulled up and found a terrified young man and his frightened wife begging for help. The man was clutching a carving knife and a screwdriver to defend himself. It was David and Maureen Smith.

They were taken to Hyde police station. There they blurted out a horrific story of murdered children, guns and axe attacks to startled detectives.

Superintendent Bob Talbot was sure something was seriously wrong at the Brady house. Smith was still shaking in terror from the bloody slaying he had witnessed just a few hours before.

Talbot decided to investigate. He was particularly worried about the talk of guns in the house. If police came openly to the door it might provoke a bloody confrontation. So, disguised as a baker's roundsman, complete with a basket of loaves, Superintendent Talbot knocked at the back door of the house at 8.40 in the morning. Hindley, who was getting ready to leave for work, opened the door.

The unarmed officer, backed up by a burly sergeant, quickly pushed past her into the house, In the front room they found Brady lying on a sofa bed in his pyjamas, writing a sick note to his boss explaining he had sprained his ankle.

Locked room

Upstairs they found a locked bedroom. When Brady was asked to open it he was reluctant to do so. When the officers told him to open it or they would kick it down, he gave way. There on the floor, trussed with string, was the butchered body of Edward Evans. The detectives quickly found the axe in a brown carrier bag. In a box nearby where Brady's Webley and Smith & Wesson handguns, fully loaded.

Brady was arrested and charged with murder. Hindley was taken in for questioning, but it would be another five days before she was charged with murder.

At first detectives found no immediate clues about other murders, but as one CID man mused over a list of names in an exercise book belonging to Brady one name jumped out at him. John Kilbride.

He was the young lad who had mysteriously vanished from the Ashton market two years before. If Brady had killed Kilbride, could he have murdered Lesley Ann Downey and Keith Bennett as well? At Brady's house the detectives soon found something else interesting. A huge collection of photographs. Some were of Hindley and her pet dogs. Some were rather badly done home pornography staring Hindley and Brady. But there were scores of scenes of the moors between Manchester and Leeds. Why?

Smith had already told them Brady had taken him there for target practice with his revolvers and had also claimed to him to have hidden the bodies of his murder victims there.

Mysterious tape

There was also a strange tape recording. In it a woman, Hindley, read out loud to a young girl the newspaper reports about the hunt for the missing girl called Lesley Ann Downey. The police asked for the help of the BBC to enhance the tapes, eradicating static and background noise. They had to find out who the little girl was.

Within days they had the answer. It was a young neighbour of Myra Hindley, who had been taken for a ride to Saddleworth Moor on Christmas Eve, 1964, just two days before Lesley Ann's body had been taken there to be buried. She showed detectives the spot where she had been taken. The area tallied closely with the area pointed out to them by David Smith, who had been to the moors to practice shooting with Brady's guns.

A huge search if the area was ordered using 150 officers and tracker dogs. They were told to look for any signs of the ground having been disturbed or dug over. On 16 October 1965 a constable made a startling discovery. There was a length of white bone sticking up from the soil. It was a human arm bone, part of Lesley's remains. Her body, naked, lay less than two feet down, close to the A635 road from Holmfirth to Greenfield. Her clothes were piled at her feet.

But could the detectives link her murder with Hindley and Brady?

Police breakthrough

Two day's later detectives were to get the breakthrough that was to sink the Moors killers once and for all. An officer checking though a prayer book belonging to Hindley entitled The Garden of the Soul found two left luggage receipts hidden in the spine.

The murder team remembered that Smith had explained how Brady had taken suitcases of belongings he considered might incriminate him to the left luggage lockers of Manchester's Central Station on the eve of every murder. Brady saw it as a form of insurance against the police finding anything at home should he be arrested while actually committing a murder.

Within hours the squad had found the cases. They contained a gold mine on information. There was the paraphernalia of armed robbery, coshes, wigs, masks, details of banks, spare ammunition for Brady's guns. There were books about sadism and torture, and amateurish photos of Hindley in obscene poses. There were scores more pictures taken on the moors, some featuring Hindley and the couple's two dogs. But the worst was yet to come.

There were pictures of a young girl, about 10-years old, naked, gagged, being subjected to vile sex abuse. And there were spools of tape.

The tapes contained the pitiful sounds of Lesley Ann Downey being subjected to her ordeal by Brady. For 13 minutes' detectives listened as she sobbed and begged Brady to let her go, implored him to stop molesting her, and pleaded for her life. At the end of the recording hardened officers who thought they had seen it all, wept openly. The tape was later to provide the most devastating evidence ever produced in an English court of law.

Meanwhile the search of the moors for more graves continued, aided by the albums of scenic shots from Brady's own collection.

Five days after the discovery of Lesley's remains, on 21 October, they were rewarded when they found the grave of John Kilbride. He had been buried, on the opposite side of the A635 stream bed, about 400 yards from Lesley Ann. The detectives realised that one picture in the Brady collection, of Hindley and her dogs sitting on top of an earthy mound, was in fact of her sitting on John Kilbride's grave.

The search for bodies continued, but by November weather conditions on the moors grew so atrocious that the police could not continue. Detectives decided they had enough to charge both Brady and Hindley with murdering all three of the victims whose bodies had been discovered; Edward Evans, John Kilbride and Lesley Ann Downey.

The trial began at Chester Assizes, held in the city's famous castle, beginning on 19 April 1966. At their previous court hearing before magistrates in Manchester scores of police had struggled to hold back a crowd of hundreds of ordinary men and women baying for the blood of the Moors Monsters.

Public hatred

In jail on remand both had to be held in solitary confinement under permanent guard after other prisoners swore they would lynch them. Their food was even tested for poison before being brought from the kitchens. No killers in Britain in modern times have caused such a storm of hatred among the general public.

Former Detective Superintendent Joe Mounsey of Lancashire police who worked on the case said: "The public hatred for them had to be experienced to be believed. There were serious worries about them being got at before they even stood trial. If the mob had got to them there is no doubt they would have ripped Brady and Hindley limb from limb."

Following anonymous threats to shoot them even as they stood trial, the dock surrounding the couple was encased in four-inch thick, bullet-proof glass.

When asked to swear on the Bible they refused to do so, saying they were atheists. Both pleaded not guilty to all the charges.

Despite fierce prosecution questioning from the Attorney General, Sir Frederick Elwyn-Jones QC, both Brady and Hindley stuck to their guns, and denied any involvement. He took the witness stand for eight hours, she for six. Both tried to shift the blame to David Smith, the man who had finally turned them in and who was now chief witness for the prosecution.

In his summing up, the judge, Mr Justice Fenton Atkinson, told the jury: "If what the prosecution had said is right then you are dealing with two sadistic killers of the utmost depravity … could anyone be as wicked as that?

It took the jury only a few hours to decide that Brady and Hindley were indeed as wicked as that. They found them unanimously guilty on all charges bar one. They accepted that Hindley had not killed John Kilbride. Brady was guilty of all three murders, Hindley to the murders of Evans and Lesley Ann, and to harbouring her lover after the murder of John Kilbride.

He was sentenced to three terms of life, she to two of life imprisonment plus seven years for the harbouring sentence. Hanging for murder had been abolished only a few months earlier.

With huge crowds still howling for instant vengeance outside the court, they were whisked away in armoured prison vans, he to Durham jail, she to the women's jail at Holloway, London. Neither would never see each other ever again and are likely to never be released.

Return to the Moors

Such was the public interest in the case that the couple were rarely out of the news in the years that followed. Hindley in particular regularly hit the front pages of the tabloid press.

In 1972 there was a hue and cry when the Governor of Holloway jail took her for a walk to Hampstead Heath. Then, two years later, there was another sensation when she appeared at the Old Bailey charged with plotting to escape in a plan arranged by a female prison officer who had become her lesbian lover. She was convicted and given another 12-month sentence.

Both she and Brady became friendly with the prison reform campaigner Lord Longford, and at least five books were published about their lives.

Throughout all Hindley had still maintained she was innocent and that she had just been an innocent dupe under the spell of her evil boyfriend.

In 1979 she wrote a 30,000-word document to the Home Secretary in support of her request for parole in which she claimed again that she had merely been an innocent and impressionable young girl who had fallen under the influence of an evil monster and was now being punished for the crimes she had little to do with. Her parole plea was turned down amid howls of fury from the media that it should ever have been ever considered.

And each time a story broke there was that picture, the one taken after her arrest, her pinched pale face, unkempt bleached blonde hair, and mad eyes staring into the camera.

Brady too was regularly in the news. He was moved from jail to Broadmoor maximum security mental hospital amid rumours that he was now completely mad. He was later moved to a similar establishment at Broad Green in Liverpool.

Brady's confession

It was there in 1985 that the second extraordinary chapter of the Moors Murderers case began. Brady was visited by a leading investigative journalist, Fred Harrison. In a series of interviews Brady confessed for the first time to his crimes, and admitted to the murders of Pauline Reade and Keith Bennett.

After the story of Brady's confession broke in a Sunday newspaper, Detective Chief Superintendent Peter Topping, head of Manchester's CID, decided to see if there was a strong enough reason to reopen the case.

Topping was a local man. He had been born in the same area of Manchester as Hindley and had been a young constable when the case first broke. He applied for permission to visit Brady, but when he got to Broad Green mental hospital he found the killer wild-eyed, ranting, abusive and uncooperative.

Topping knew he could get nowhere with Brady in this frame of mind. Instead he tried a different tack. He went to see Myra Hindley, who was by now 44, at Cookham Wood woman's prison in Kent. Topping believed the bodies of Pauline Reade and Keith Bennett were still out on the moors and he now appealed to Myra Hindley to help him find them.

Hindley had been much affected by a letter she had received from Keith Bennett's mother appealing to her to help police find his body and put her out of the agony she had suffered for over 20 years, not knowing what had happened to her son.

Topping showed Hindley dozens of pictures of Hollin Brow Knoll and Shiny Brook, a stream running across the moor, taken by Brady. The bodies of John Kilbride and Lesley Ann Downey had been buried close to these locations.

The policeman and the murderess talked for many hours. Hindley said she could not point out anything from the pictures but was prepared to go back to the scene with the police.

Before she went back, on 16 December 1986, Topping paid another visit to Brady. He found him a changed man. Instead of the ranting madman he had met before, Brady was calm and polite, but said he did not want to offer any more help.

Searching for the bodies

Very special arrangements were made for Hindley. The press had been alerted and sums of up to £50,000 were being offered for a picture. There were other worries. There were plenty of people who would still have liked to kill Hindley and the police decided to give her an armed escort.

The police helicopter touched down on the specially closed off A635 from swirling banks of grey clouds. There was snow on the ground as Hindley, dressed in a black anorak, rubber boots and a blue balaclava, stepped out, closely escorted by two female prison officers. There they were met by Topping and other officers in a Land Rover.

For hours the party stumbled about in driving snow as Hindley tried to retrace the steps she had taken with her murderous boyfriend 24 years before. Several times she said she thought they were close to the right area, but although the craggy fell had changed little in the quarter century, her memory for the exact locations had dimmed and she became disorientated and confused.

With darkness closing in the effort was called off and Hindley was taken back to Kent. By the end of the week the weather was so bad the search was abandoned altogether.

As a final throw of the dice, Topping had David Smith brought up to the moor to see if he could recognise and land mark shown to him by Brady. But it was all to no avail.

Topping continued to see Hindley after Christmas. Their rapport was growing. The detective felt that Hindley was on the point of making a huge decision. By February 1987 his hunch was proved correct. After 21 years in jail steadfastly protesting her innocence, Hindley wanted to confess everything. Over two days she allowed police to tape record 17 hours of her own terrible story.

In March Topping asked the Home Office for permission to take Hindley back to Saddleworth Moor. With nothing more for her to hide he was sure she would now do her utmost to pinpoint the last resting places of Pauline Reade and Keith Bennett. Later that month the permission came through. This time the media did not get wind of the visit.

Again Hindley spent hours tramping through the pot holes and heather of the craggy hills. Again, her efforts were fruitless. Topping decided the search much go on. Despite criticism from some quarters, he was certain there were bodies there.

Police were now able to call on the kind of specialist aid they had not had in the 1960s. Archaeologists and geologists gave advice on how to look for changes in soil and rock formations. Botanist's advised on how sudden changes in patterns of vegetation might indicate a grave site. The RAF photographed the whole area from the air so accurate comparisons could be made between the features in Brady's snaps at the time of the murders and those of 25 years on.

Third grave found

It was not until 1 July 1987 that police made their incredible find. In the early afternoon a search team exploring a piece of ground about 150 yards from the road noticed a difference in the vegetation. After a few minutes of careful digging the heel of a white shoe was uncovered. It was the grave of Pauline Reade. Her body had been remarkably well preserved by the peaty soil. Her shoes had been new on the day she died.

In the days before Pauline's body was discovered Chief Superintendent Topping had started a fresh dialogue with Brady. Brady enjoyed the attention and liked playing games with the police. He said he would be happy to confess and lead them to the bodies if he was given the means to kill himself afterwards.

He volunteered to go to Saddleworth Moor himself, if he could have a whole week away from the mental hospital that caged him and if he could have his own choice of food and alcohol to drink.

When news of the discovery of Pauline Reade's body broke Brady said he wanted to go back to the moor urgently, to show police Keith Bennett's last resting place and to have done with the whole affair.

Topping already had permission from the Home Office to take Brady to the moors. He took him the next day, 3 July 1987.

For 12 hours Brady, dishevelled and wearing dark glasses, stumbled about the moor with the detectives trying to get his bearings. In the end he failed. Like his former lover, his memory had faded.

Later Brady said he wanted to tell Topping about five other murders he had committed. In lengthy interviews he claimed to have clubbed a man to death with a brick in Manchester, shot an 18-year old and buried his body on Saddleworth Moor, and thrown a woman to her death from a canal bridge in Manchester. He had also stabbed a man he saw molesting a woman by a canal in Glasgow and shot a young male hiker whom he had stopped on a lonely road in Loch Lomond.

In the end it was impossible for the police to substantiate whether these murder stories were true or just fantasies from the twisted mind of Ian Brady.

Laid to rest

Pauline Reade was given a proper funeral on 7 August 1987. On 24 August Topping called off the search for the body of Keith Bennett. A decision was made that there was no point in setting a new trial for the killers over Pauline Reade.

Topping kept the dialogue going between him and the Moors Murderers, ever hopeful that some new clue might emerge. By December 1987 Brady wanted to go back to the moors again.

On 8 December he was taken back for a few hours to tramp about in areas he said were significant but that police had already searched in great detail. The search for Keith Bennett was finally called off completely. But Chief Superintendent Topping still believes there is at least one body still buried. He said before he retired; "I am sure he's still out there somewhere."

END

Milton Keynes UK
Ingram Content Group UK Ltd.
UKHW030834021124
450589UK00002B/403